Mystery Guest at the House of Fun

Jon Blake

illustrated by
David Roberts

Hodder
Children's
Books

A division of Hodder Headline Limited

A Catalogue record for this book is available from the British Library

ISBN 0 340 88461 4

Printed and bound in Great Britain by
Bookmarque Ltd, Croydon, Surrey

The paper and board used in this paperback by Hodder Children's Books
are natural recyclable products made from wood grown in sustainable
forests. The manufacturing processes conform to the environmental
regulations of the country of origin.

Hodder Children's Books
A division of Hodder Headline Limited
338 Euston Road, London NW1 3BH

Before We Begin

First let me introduce myself. I am Blue Soup. I tell stories. I also light up cities, provide hot dinners, and make that little thing in the top of the toilet go FZZZZZZZ. In fact, I make everything work, so no one has to waste their time being a cleaner, or an estate agent, or an MP.

What am I, you ask? Well, I'm not a person, that's obvious. Or a team of people. Or a computer virus. But please don't waste your time trying to imagine me, because you can't, just like you can't imagine the end of time, or what's beyond the very last star. If you do try to imagine me, first you will get a headache, then your head will explode.

As you've probably guessed, I come from Outer Space. Beyond the very last star, in fact. I was brought here by what you call aliens, except to them, you are aliens, and pretty weird ones at that.

Anyway, enough of me. This is the third story of Stinky Finger, who was first described in Stinky Finger's House of Fun. As you may know, there are no grown-ups in Stinky's world. They've all been sucked up into the Space Zoo by the Spoonheads. That's why Stinky and his friends are in charge of the House of Fun, where something mad or dangerous is always around the corner …

… as you will soon see.

Chapter One

It was just another day at the House of Fun. Stinky sat in his favourite armchair, wearing his best suit and tie. His hair was neatly parted and there was a faint whiff of lavender rising from his freshly scrubbed face.

"Do you know, Icky," he said, "I really prefer the spearmint toothpaste. The peppermint never seems to get my teeth quite as sparkly."

Icky Bats viewed his great mate curiously. He knew there was something slightly wrong about him, but couldn't quite work out what it was. Was it the carefully clipped fingernails? The perfectly clean shirt collar? Or was it those teeth, even and white and actually very sparkly indeed?

Suddenly Icky became aware of an urgent tug at

11

his elbow. A voice seemed to come from nowhere. "Icky!" it said. "Bryan's rung the gong!"

Icky tried to reply, but no words would come. The vision of Stinky before him slowly dissolved, to be replaced by a new one, much closer and much smellier. The new Stinky had yellow teeth, chocolate stains on his nose and matted hair full of all manner of wildlife.

"Wake up, Icky!" urged the new Stinky.

Icky sat up, just in time to see a juicy green maggot drop off Stinky's head into his lap.

"I've just had a weird dream," said Icky. "It was you, except it was the opposite of you."

"That's funny," said Stinky. "I've just dreamt about you, except you thought before you did things."

"We must stop sleeping in the Cheesy Dreams Bedroom," said Icky.

Note from Blue Soup:

The Cheesy Dreams Bedroom, of course, was one of the many weird rooms in the House of Fun, the house which Stinky looked after for his uncle Nero, whose frozen head was outside in the mailbox. If all this is new to you, try reading Stinky Finger's House of Fun. On second thoughts, don't – it might put you off reading this one.

"Anyway," said Stinky, "we'd better get downstairs for breakfast. You know what Bryan's like."

Icky groaned. Besides being a brain-box, Bryan Brain liked to get things organised – very organised. Bryan had given everybody a Project Book and a

Timetable, so that the House of Fun could be more like school. The Timetable said everyone should be up at 8.30 a.m. for breakfast, which was why Bryan rang a big gong at 8.25 precisely.

As Icky and Stinky arrived in the kitchen, they could see that all was not well. Bryan was standing next to an open cupboard, drumming his fingers, with a very severe look on his face.

"Something up, Bry?" said Icky.

"It seems," said Bryan sternly, "we have a thief."

"What kind of thief?" asked Stinky.

"A malted milk biscuit thief," replied Bryan.

"Oh," said Stinky. "What's he stolen?"

"What do you think he's stolen?" railed Bryan.

"Jewellery?" suggested Stinky.

"Malted milk biscuits!" snapped Bryan. "*Three* of my malted milk biscuits!"

Obviously this was very serious. Bryan treasured his packets of malted milk biscuits. He ate one at breakfast dipped in a cup of tea, and one at supper dipped in hot strawberry milk. Bryan always knew exactly how many biscuits he had in his cupboard, which was why he was now sure he was three short.

"I never took 'em," said Icky. "They taste like sick."

"Aha!" said Bryan. "How do you know they taste like sick?"

"You gave me one once," replied Icky. "For my birthday."

"Ah yes," said Bryan, suddenly remembering this generous act of long-ago.

All eyes turned to Stinky.

"Shall we have breakfast now?" said Stinky.

"Certainly not!" said Bryan. "No one shall eat till we find out who stole my malted milk biscuits!"

"How are we going to do that?" asked Icky.

"We are going to search every room in this house," replied Bryan, "until we find crumbs."

This seemed like a waste of time to Icky. Bryan only had to look in Stinky's hair to find at least five years' worth of crumbs, and there was no way of knowing if they were malted milk, bread, cream cracker, or scabby nit-nests. But Icky didn't say anything, because he'd been bored lately, and this seemed like an adventure.

"It's a long walk," said Stinky, "all round the house."

15

"We're not walking," replied Bryan. "We're going on the metro."

"Metro?" said Stinky. "What metro?"

"Aha!" said Bryan, tapping his tap-like nose knowingly.

Icky and Stinky followed Bryan into the hall, then down the steps in to the cellar. As you may know, the three mates had only recently ventured into this part of the house. They'd thought it was called Satan's Crypt, and only just before Christmas realised it was actually *Santa's* Crypt, and really quite pleasant.

Santa's Crypt was now looking a bit worn down. The remains of the Christmas party were scattered everywhere. Bryan ignored all this and marched straight to the large sign in the corner of the room marked:

GM

He pulled a lever on the wall beneath the sign, a sliding door opened, and an escalator appeared, going down.

"Frabjous!" said Icky.

"I've seen those signs all round the house," said Stinky. "I always wondered what they meant."

"What *do* they mean?" asked Icky.

"You'll find out," replied Bryan. He could have told them, of course, but Bryan was enjoying his little moment of power.

The three great mates set off down the escalator. It was a strange thing to find that the cellar had a cellar, and maybe another cellar below that. After all, the House of Fun was perched on a hill, so the possibilities were endless.

At the bottom of the escalator was a surprisingly

large hall, lit in a ghostly green light. Immediately ahead were three rusting metal turnstiles, and on the left a wooden booth with a sign saying TICKET OFFICE, except the lights weren't working properly and it looked more like TICK OFF.

"It's freezing down here!" said Stinky. He thought about hugging himself but feared his arms might get stuck to his shirt.

Icky gasped as he suddenly realised something. "Stinky!" he cried. "You're not wearing Old Faithful!"

Old Faithful was Stinky's favourite jumper. Stinky always wore Old Faithful on Tuesdays, Thursdays and Saturdays, and also on Mondays, Wednesdays and Fridays. That only left Sundays, of course, except it didn't really leave Sundays, because he also wore it then.

Stinky looked down, a little puzzled, then something dawned on him. "I took it off at bedtime," he said.

"Took it off at bedtime?" repeated Icky. "Why?"

"It was keeping me awake," replied Stinky.

"Keeping you awake?" repeated Bryan. "How can a jumper keep you awake?"

"It moved about," replied Stinky.

Icky nodded. "There was a lot of animal life in it," he said.

Stinky shivered again. "Can we stop at the Cheesy Dreams bedroom?" he asked. "I'd like to put it back on."

Bryan smiled a secret smile. "Sure," he said. "But first … you'll need a ticket." He ushered Stinky towards the ticket office. Stinky sauntered innocently towards it, then just as he arrived at the little window, leapt back like he'd been shot.

There, behind a wire grille, wearing a faded peaked cap, was a luminous grinning skeleton.

Brian guffawed loudly. "Did I forget to mention?" he said. "It's a *ghost* train! *GM*, see? Ghost Metro!" Suddenly, however, his smile faded. "What's that smell?" he said.

"I've been to the toilet a bit," replied Stinky.

"Eeurgh!" said Bryan. "Change your pants!"

"No thanks," said Stinky. "Nice and warm now."

"Let's go!" said Icky, who always wanted to do everything straight away, and if possible earlier.

Stinky scratched his head. "If we can't get a ticket," he asked, "how do we get in?"

"Like this!" said Icky, leaping over the turnstile.

"Do you think we're supposed to do that?" asked Stinky.

"Who's going to stop us?" said Icky. He pointed at the skeleton in the ticket booth. "Him?"

Everybody laughed, then Stinky and Bryan also jumped over the turnstile.

Suddenly, however, a kind of drawbridge dropped out of the wall with a thunderous THUNK. Behind it was a seven-foot bandaged mummy wearing a tattered *GM* cap. It clunked out of its hidey-hole and bore down on the three mates with slow inevitable steps. Each jarring step sent a small shudder through its rigid body, and a much larger shudder through the three mates.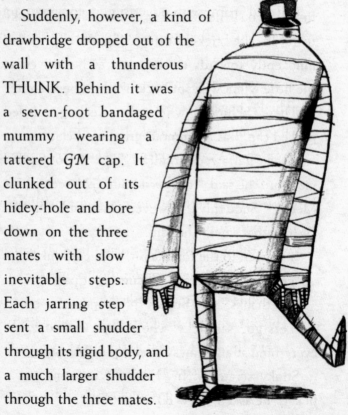

"Run!" cried Icky, but Bryan was already gone. Stinky followed, down a dim tunnel, towards a sign saying Platform 1 – Eastbound. Platform 2 – The other way.

Bryan went for Platform 1. The others raced after him, finding themselves at last beside the metro line. Everything seemed old and faded and worn, with adverts from long-ago and cracked old marble tiles. There was no sign of a train.

"Hurry!" squealed Bryan.

The PA began to crackle.

"It's coming!" yelled Icky.

From the PA came a deep, long and very chilling laugh.

Meanwhile a certain someone had joined them on the platform.

"Wait till he's close," said Bryan, "then all leap at him together and push him on the live rail."

"Which is the live rail?" asked Icky.

"The one with the fried rats on it," replied Bryan.

"I don't think I can do it," said Stinky.

"You've got to!" squealed Bryan.

By now the steps were so close the three mates

21

could almost smell the putrid flesh of the killer mummy. Closer, and closer, and …

… it stopped.

The mummy was frozen in mid-stride, about a metre from Icky's left leg.

"W-what happened?" asked Stinky.

"I think his batteries ran out," said Bryan.

"If we warm them up in our hands," said Icky eagerly, "we might get a bit more life out of them."

"Icky," said Bryan, "is that something we really want to do?"

Icky hung his head. "Just an idea," he mumbled.

At this point there was a whooshing sound, a gust of wind and a rumble. Suddenly the ghost metro train rushed from the tunnel. The three mates weren't sure what was at the controls, except that it didn't have a head but was doing a good job in the circumstances.

The train pulled in and the doors slid open. The carriage was crowded out with ghouls, zombies, werewolves and a wide range of the living dead, but that didn't put Icky off. He jumped straight on.

"Get on, you two!" he shouted. "They're only models!"

Stinky didn't think they *looked* like models and couldn't imagine any of them on a catwalk, but he trusted Icky in all things, usually unwisely. He climbed aboard and was followed by Bryan, who was still trying to act confident, but not very convincingly.

The train doors closed and the train set off. Icky looked perfectly happy, sitting amongst the frozen zombies, but Bryan was looking increasingly anxious. He had become painfully aware he was in a Public Place. Ever since he had had a certain dream, Bryan had had serious problems with Public Places.

"Icky," he said. "Can you just look down … and check I've got trousers on?"

"Yes, Bryan," replied Icky, wearily. "You've got trousers on."

Bryan looked relieved, but not for long. The train hurtled into a long dark tunnel, with all manner of sudden ghastly sights looming up outside the windows. The journey seemed to take forever.

"How come this tunnel's so long," asked Stinky, "when the house is quite short?"

"It must be like an anthill," grunted Bryan.

"Aha," said Stinky, who had no idea what an anthill was, but didn't fancy a half-hour lecture.

Icky, meanwhile, was whistling happily to himself and studying the map of the Ghost Metro. It was unusual for Icky to read a map as he was usually on his way before he even knew where he

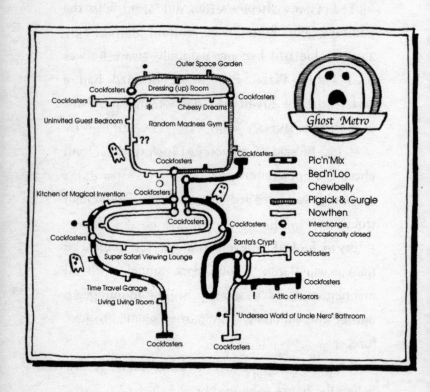

was going. But the metro map was bright and colourful and full of interesting names.

"Cheesy Dreams," he announced. "Last stop on the Bed'n'loo line before Cockfosters."

"What's Cockfosters?" asked Stinky.

"There's always a Cockfosters at the end of a metro line," replied Bryan knowingly.

The Ghost Metro really did seem like the slowest way of getting around the House of Fun. The three mates had to change lines three times and go up or down at least five escalators before they finally reached the sign which said EXIT – CHEE AMS. SY DRE was covered up by something green and dead with its eyeballs hanging out, but by now the three mates didn't take much notice. They emerged gratefully behind the fridge in the corner of the cheesy dreams bedroom and Bryan got straight to work with his magnifying glass.

"This is stupid," said Icky. "Even if you do find a crumb, how do you know it's a malted milk crumb?"

"Instincts," replied Bryan.

Stinky wasn't sure what In-stinks were, but he liked the sound of them. He'd heard of In-soles, which made your feet smell better, and figured that In-stinks probably made them smell worse.

"Aha!" said Bryan, picking up a small green object. "What is this?"

"That's not a malted milk crumb!" replied Icky. "It's a gherkin!"

"But what is it doing in the bedroom?" asked Bryan.

"It probably fell out of Old Faithful," replied Icky.

"Old Faithful!" repeated Stinky. "That reminds me!"

Stinky went to retrieve his beloved jumper, while Bryan carried on combing the scene of the suspected crime. He found another gherkin, half a scotch egg and three toenails. He was just about to investigate a suspicious woodlouse when there was a gasp from Stinky.

"Old Faithful!" he cried. "It's gone!"

Chapter Two

Note from Blue Soup:

We're now about to carry on from exactly where we left off. We only stopped because it was a dramatic moment which cried out for a dramatic pause. In the old days, before the Spoonheads, there were lots of these moments on TV (especially American TV), which were a good excuse for an "ad break". "Ad breaks" were full of things called "ads" which tried to make you buy things, in the days before money was abolished. An example follows. Try to imagine a deep dark voice with an American accent and lots of pictures of attractive people in interesting situations.

*IN A WORLD WHERE GROWN-UPS ARE
LOST FOREVER*

*THREE YOUNG HEROES COME TO A
HOUSE OF DREAMS*

*AND FIND THEIR ULTIMATE
NIGHTMARE*

Stinky: What the bleep is it out there?

*Icky: I don't know, pal ... but I don't think
it's come to wish us happy birthday!*

Bryan opens the front door. His face falls.

Bryan: NO-O-O-O-O-O-O-O-O-O-O!

*THE STINKY TRILOGY
NOW AVAILABLE ON DVD, ZBZ AND
GROUPSOUP*

And now back to the story.

Bryan viewed Stinky doubtfully. "Are you *sure* that's where you left Old Faithful, Stinky?" he asked.

"Definitely," replied Stinky. "I put it by the bed in case I got lonely in the night."

Stinky did not often sound this sure about something. Icky was puzzled.

"Who'd want to steal Old Faithful?" he asked.

"Someone with no taste," said Bryan.

"Or sense of smell," added Icky.

Bryan wheeled on Icky. "You!" he said. "You've got no sense of smell!"

It was true. As everybody knows, Icky was once hit on the nose by a cricket ball, which was why he had become Stinky's only friend.

"I wouldn't steal anything off Stinky!" said Icky.

"Aha!" said Bryan. "Then you *would* steal something off *me*!"

"I never said that!" protested Icky.

"Exactly!" said Bryan. "You never said it because then we would know you were guilty!"

"Right!" said Icky, who by now was hopping

from one foot to the other. "Give me a lie detector test, and then we'll see if I'm guilty!"

"Right!" said Bryan. "I will!"

"Right!" said Icky.

"Right!" said Bryan.

A small uncertain frown crossed Icky's brow. "Have we got a lie detector?" he asked.

Bryan also frowned. He pressed a thoughtful finger to his lips. He looked to the left. He looked to the right. "There might be something in the museum," he said finally.

The museum wasn't really a museum. It was Bryan's collection of electronic bits and pieces. Bryan had been collecting electronic bits and pieces since the age of 0, for no particular reason except he liked collecting, and liked electronic bits and pieces. He did once announce a plan to turn the House of Fun into the National Museum of Electronic Miscellany (bits and pieces), but Icky and Stinky pretended not to hear him. In fact they pretended not to hear him every day for seven weeks, until he finally shut up.

Bryan kept his Electronic Miscellany in one of the Rooms Without A Name on Floor 2.5 of the House of Fun. It was a half-minute walk from the Cheesy Dreams Bedroom, or twenty-five minutes on the Ghost Metro.

The three mates decided to walk.

Bryan certainly had a lot of bits and pieces. They were stacked four deep and took up a quarter of the room. Some of them went right back to the early twenty-first century, when computers and things were very primitive indeed.

"Is this a lie detector?" asked Icky, picking up an interesting-looking box with a keyboard on one end of it.

"Certainly not!" snapped Bryan, snatching it away. "That's an ancient Burpitron text-to-voice vocal synth module."

"What does it do?" said Icky. As we all know, Icky was easily distracted from the Job At Hand.

"It talks," grunted Bryan impatiently. He typed the word BUMBLEBEE into it, and sure enough, a flat robot voice said "**bumblebee**", except its 'b's weren't very good and it sounded more like "**numbleknee**".

"Frabjous!" cried Icky. "Let's make it swear!"

"Certainly not," said Bryan. "It's a very serious and important piece of equipment."

All Bryan's bits and pieces were serious and important, according to Bryan. But none of them was a lie detector.

"We could always get one from Yellow Mist," suggested Bryan.

"I don't like that idea," said Stinky, who'd once got lost in Yellow Mist for a fortnight.

"I do!" said Icky, who'd also got lost, but had rather enjoyed it.

"Let's vote on it," said Bryan. "All those in favour of Yellow Mist."

Bryan and Icky raised their hands. Stinky stood uncertainly for a moment, then, forgetting what the vote was about, raised his as well.

"Let's go!" cried Icky.

Note from Blue Soup:

In the olden days, before the Spoonheads came, humans had a number of ways of finding the thing they wanted. They would guess what kind of shop might sell it, then look up the name of the shop in a 'directory', then call the shop on a 'telephone', then (unbelievably) go to the shop and buy the item with money. This process could take half a day or more, and sometimes ended in complete failure. The alternative was the 'World Wide Web', a computer network invented by the American war department. Again, the human would have to find someone who sold the item, order it, and sometimes wait days for its arrival.

All this nonsense ended when Yellow Mist was installed on Earth. I won't bother to describe how it works, because you are just about to find out.

Yellow Mist would be somewhere down town. Usually it hung around in the Olde Market Square, but on a windy day it sometimes drifted down to the river. Once it got right out of town altogether and was trapped in the hills for weeks. Like a faithful dog, however, it always returned where it belonged.

Icky, Stinky and Bryan half-walked, half-ran down the hill towards town. Much as the three mates loved the House of Fun, it was good to get out of it, which was why they did this at least once a year. For Bryan, however, it was always a testing experience.

"Icky …" he began, "… could you just look down and check—"

"Yes, Bryan," said Icky tiredly. "You've got trousers on."

"There's Yellow Mist!" cried Stinky, pointing towards the park by the river.

"Well done, Stinks!" said Icky. Stinky wasn't often the one to see a thing first, or see it at all sometimes.

As usual, Yellow Mist was very thin at the edge, where you could still see fairly clearly, getting thicker and thicker towards the centre, where you couldn't see at all. It was important for the three mates to stay close together, which meant they would have to hold hands.

"I'm not holding hands with Stinky," declared Bryan.

"I'm not holding hands with Bryan," declared Icky.

"Let's elect a Leader," suggested Stinky.

Bryan agreed and proposed himself. There were no votes against. As Leader, Bryan would of course have to go in the centre, which meant that Bryan and Stinky and Icky and Bryan all ended up holding hands. Icky's hand was hot and sticky, Bryan's was cold and dry, and Stinky's was a bit like clammy old hanky, mainly because it had a clammy old hanky in it.

The three mates moved forward into the mist. As it began to thicken, they called out together: "Lie detector wanted! Lie detector wanted!"

There was no way of knowing how the lie detector might arrive. It might drop into their arms or appear in a trolley before them. It might arrive ready-packed in a back-pack which nestled on to their shoulders. But one way or another, it would come.

"Seen anything yet?" said Bryan, as they moved through the very thickest part of the mist.

"Nope," said Icky.

"Not me," said Stinky.

"Funny," said Bryan.

The three mates carried on, calling out, "Lie detector wanted!" but the mist was getting thinner, and nothing seemed to be happening. Then, just as they were about to leave the mist altogether, Icky had a strange feeling.

"Bryan," he said, "are you holding my right hand?"

"Indeed," replied Bryan.

"In that case," said Icky, "who's holding the left one?"

At this point, the three mates became able to see again. They all looked to the left. Stinky went "Uh?", Bryan went "Uhhhh!", and Icky went "URRRRRRGH!"

A very strange person was holding hands with Icky. Although, like everyone on Earth, he must have been fourteen or less, his long straggly hair was balding on top and a wispy beard hung from his chin. He was dressed in a waistcoat of many colours, above breeches which stopped at the knee, green stockings and soft green slip-on shoes. Around one knee he wore a garter of bells, which he jangled as if to say hello.

"W-who are you?" asked Bryan.

"I," replied the jangly one, "am a lie detector."

"You don't look like a lie detector," said Icky, removing his hand from the jangly one's grasp.

"How do you work?" said Bryan suspiciously.

"That," replied the jangly one, "you will find out soon enough." He laughed in a shrill and unsettling way, then began skipping merrily down the path by the river. "Follow, follow, down to the hollow!" he cried.

Not knowing what else to do, the three mates followed. The jangly one skipped and jumped, danced and hopped all the way to a sun-dappled glade in the deep depths of an ancient wood. There he sprang to face the three mates, performing a deep and dramatic bow.

"I," he declared, "am Diggory Dollop."

There was a pause.

"I'm Icky," said Icky.

"I'm Stinky," said Stinky.

"I'm fed up of this," said Bryan.

"Patience!" cried Diggory Dollop. "Soon all will be revealed."

Diggory Dollop dug into his inside pocket and produced a silver flute.

"That's not a lie detector," said Bryan.

"We shall see!" said Diggory Dollop. He placed the flute to his lips and began to play. There was a great urgency about him, particularly his left leg. The jangly bells jingled to the rhythm of his stamping foot, and the whole glade seemed to dance to his twisty melody. After a few moments Stinky was surprised to notice his own foot tapping. Icky's started up soon after, and even Bryan could not resist the magic pipe. Diggory played on, faster and faster. Bryan's legs began to weave about, Stinky's hands began to clap, and Icky's head began to nod like a frantic pecking bird.

"Are you ready for the Dance of Truth?" cried Diggory.

"Yes!" they all cried.

Diggory stopped. "Who's first?" he asked.

"Oh," said Bryan. "What about Icky?"

"All right," said Icky.

"Cover your ears," said Diggory, to Stinky and Bryan. "Then, when I command ye, ask whatsoever questions ye desire."

"Pardon?" said Stinky, who'd already covered his ears.

"It's all right, Stinky," said Bryan. "Leave it to me."

Bryan prepared himself. So did Icky, except he wasn't sure what for. Diggory raised his flute once more and began to play. This time he began quite softly, but soon built up into a wild gypsy reel, foot stamping like a piston. Icky hopped gently from foot to foot, then began rocking an imaginary baby. As the music grew more frenzied, so Icky's dance grew crazier and crazier, elbows going ten to the dozen.

"Ask ye now!" cried Diggory, nodding his head at Bryan and Stinky.

"Icky!" cried Bryan. "What do you really think of me?"

"You're a bigheaded idiot!" cried Icky.

Bryan frowned. "I see," he said. "And what do you *really* think of malted milk biscuits!?"

"They taste like sick!" cried Icky.

"So you stole them just to annoy me!" cried Bryan.

"I did not!" cried Icky.

Bryan looked disappointed. "Are you sure this is the Dance of Truth?" he asked Diggory.

Diggory stopped playing. Icky came to a standstill, then shook his head about a bit. "What happened?" he asked.

"Nothing much," replied Bryan.

"Next," said Diggory.

Bryan guided Stinky forward. Icky covered his ears. Diggory began to play a new tune, just as catchy as the one before, and Stinky was soon juddering and shuddering and doing little bunny hops this way and that. This was the way Stinky always danced, even when he wasn't in a trance.

"Ask ye now!" cried Diggory.

"Stinky Finger!" cried Bryan. "I put it to you that on the third day of July you did steal three malted milk biscuits, then, in order to cover your crime, stole your own jumper!"

"Eh?" said Stinky. Being in a trance didn't help him understand Bryan any better.

"Stinky!" yelled Icky. "Did you steal Bryan's bickies?"

"No!" cried Stinky.

"Did you steal your own jumper?" cried Icky.

"No!" cried Stinky.

"That's it then," said Icky.

Diggory lowered the flute. Stinky bunny-hopped for a few seconds, then slowly came back to his senses. "Have we started yet?" he asked.

Bryan frowned. "This can't be right," he said.

"The truth will out, in the Dance of Truth," declared Diggory.

"*Someone* stole those biscuits," said Bryan.

"Hold on a moment," said Icky. "We haven't tested you yet."

"Me?" squealed Bryan. "How can I have stolen my own biscuits?"

"You might have been sleepwalking," suggested Stinky.

"You might have taken the biscuits so we wouldn't suspect you when you stole Old Faithful," suggested Icky.

"Eh?" said Stinky.

"Poppycock!" cried Bryan.

"Eh?" said Stinky.

"Come on, Bryan," said Icky. "Everyone must dance the Dance of Truth."

Bryan protested loudly, but Diggory agreed with Icky, and Stinky agreed with whatever Diggory was agreeing with. Bryan had no choice but to take his place on the grassy dancefloor. "No laughing," he said solemnly, which was quite funny in itself.

Diggory stamped his jangly leg and once more took up his magic flute. You could sense Bryan resisting, resisting, resisting, feet planted square on the ground and teeth gritted like the jaws of a vice. As the music grew wilder, however, his legs began to quiver, his eyes began to water, until he could stand it no more. Bryan flew into a jig, like a bonkers piglet on hot coals. He was wilder than Stinky, wilder than Icky, even wilder than the well wild Diggory.

There was no doubt about it. Bryan was ready to spill the beans.

Icky nudged Stinky. "Let's ask him if he eats bogeys," he suggested.

"That's not really fair," said Stinky.

Icky looked downcast. "We've got to ask him *something* funny," he said.

"Let's just ask him what he asked us," suggested Stinky.

"All right," said Icky, with a sigh. "Bryan!" he yelled. "What do you really think of us?"

Bryan began to pant. He seemed to be building up to something. "I ..." he began. "I ... love you!"

"Eh?" said Stinky.

"Eh?" said Icky.

"I've never had friends before!" cried Bryan. "You've made me so ... happy!"

Icky and Stinky went as red as tomatoes. But Bryan wasn't finished.

"I just don't know how to show how much I love you!" he cried. "That's why I boss you about!"

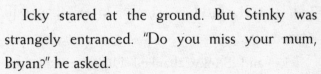

Icky stared at the ground. But Stinky was strangely entranced. "Do you miss your mum, Bryan?" he asked.

"Yes!" cried Bryan, with a heartfelt sob. "That's why I ... I ... I ... eat the biscuits!"

"Did you take your own biscuits, Bryan?" asked Stinky.

There was a dramatic pause.

"No," said Bryan. "I didn't do that."

Stinky had many, many more questions for Bryan. Usually Stinky had one idea a year, but the Dance of Truth had set his brain alive. Stinky got so lost in the conversation, he didn't notice two hours passing, by which time Bryan was starting to flag quite badly.

"I think he's had enough," said Stinky.

"Hold on," said Icky. "Just one more question."

"Just one then," said Stinky.

Icky's face became deadly serious. "Bryan," he said. "Have you ever eaten a bogey?"

At this point Diggory stopped playing. The reel had come to an end, and that was Bryan's time over. Bryan staggered to a nearby tree stump and slumped down. He could not understand why he was so tired, yet oddly relaxed.

Icky and Stinky thanked Diggory, who put away his flute and skipped back towards Yellow Mist, job done.

"You didn't steal the biscuits, by the way," Stinky told Bryan.

"Of course I didn't," snapped Bryan.

"But if it wasn't one of us," said Icky, "who was it?"

A chill suddenly descended on the glade. The sun had gone in, and the wood seemed full of dangers.

"Someone, or some *thing* must be in the House of Fun – something that stole my biscuits," declared Bryan. His voice had gone quite quivery.

"It'll be OK, Bryan," said Stinky. He tried to land a reassuring paw on Bryan's shoulder, but Bryan ducked away.

Icky and Stinky gave each other a knowing smile.

"Let's get back, and find it, and kill it!" said Icky.

The three mates made their way back to the House of Fun. Bryan headed straight for his biscuits, to check no more had gone. "Thank heaven for that," he said. He decided to take the biscuits back to his room and put them in the safe with all his certificates.

"What a day," said Stinky. "Shall we have a cup of tea?"

Suddenly there was an anguished yell from upstairs. "The Burpitron text-to-voice vocal synth module!" cried Bryan. "It's gone!"

Chapter Three

Bryan paced the kitchen, biting his nails. "We've got to stay calm," he said.

Icky and Stinky, who were quite calm, urged Bryan to sit down. He was making them dizzy.

"Maybe it's the zombies," suggested Icky.

"Pah!" said Bryan, sitting down. "They're not real!"

"But there's no one else in the house," said Icky. "Just us, and …"

"… Dronezone!" cried Bryan, leaping up again.

"Dronezone!" repeated Icky, leaping up as well.

"Dronezone are potatoes," muttered Stinky. "They can't climb stairs."

Icky sat down again. "That's true," he said.

"In fact," added Stinky, "they can't even walk."

As far as we know," said Bryan, who, as usual, was suspicious of everyone, even boy bands who had been turned into root vegetables.

Note from Blue Soup:

Most of you are probably aware that Dronezone were once the world's biggest male vocal group. They'd come to stay at the House of Fun some years before and made the mistake of watching telly in the Living Living Room. This telly unfortunately had a habit of watching back, and turning people into potatoes.

Unknown to the three mates, Dronezone had now recruited a fifth member, despite being potatoes.

General Pig, who had once led an army of pigs against the house, was also now a potato. The Dronezone boys had discovered he had a very fine voice (though, like them, a tiny tinny one). They'd been secretly rehearsing at night and were planning to release a track together called Ham and Mash MegaMix.

"I've just had a thought," said Stinky.

"Yes!?" cried Icky and Bryan, amazedly.

There was a dramatic pause.

"No," said Stinky. "Gone again."

Icky leapt up for a second time. "I've just had one, now!" he cried.

"Go on," said Stinky.

"Why don't we ask Dronezone if they've heard anything?" said Icky. "They'd be sure to hear if someone was in the kitchen, or came through the front door."

"Yes," said Stinky. "Let's do that."

"Hrmmm," said Bryan, but only because he hadn't thought of it.

As usual, Dronezone were on the sofa, not doing much, although General Pig did seem to have moved a little closer to the others.

"They're looking guilty," said Bryan, but no one took much notice.

"I'll talk to them," said Icky.

Icky perched on the edge of the sofa and tried not to look too threatening. Icky was best at talking to Dronezone, because their voices were so very tiny and high-pitched, and the others could never quite pick up their wavelength.

"Boys," said Icky. "I need to ask you a Serious Question."

Dronezone were all ears, despite being 100% potato.

"Boys," asked Icky. "I want you to tell me if you've heard any Strange Noises in the Night."

"Or the day," added Bryan.

"Such as Footsteps, or Biscuit Nibbling, or Guilty Sniggering," added Icky.

A tiny chorus of excited chittering came from the World's Greatest Boy Band. Icky strained to listen. His face took on many different expressions, enough to make Bryan and Stinky quite worried.

"What is it?" hissed Bryan.

"They have heard something," replied Icky, "but it wasn't footsteps. It was a strange swishing sound, like curtains being dragged over a marble floor."

"A ghost!" cried Bryan, with a tremble.

"It does sound like a ghost," agreed Icky.

"I knew it!" cried Bryan.

"Oh dear," said Stinky.

"Maybe if we set up some cameras," suggested Icky, "we could catch it."

"Nit!" said Bryan. "You can't catch a ghost on camera."

"I thought that was a vampire," said Icky.

"We need a dog," said Stinky.

Everything went quiet for a moment as Icky and Bryan struggled to follow Stinky's line of thought.

"Need a dog, Stinky?" muttered Icky.

"Dogs can tell when there's a ghost," said Stinky. "They whine."

"That's right!" said Icky, much impressed.

Bryan sighed. "Have you forgotten?" he said. "Dogs are troublemakers. They've been trouble-makers ever since the stupid Spoonheads taught them to talk."

That was true. But Icky was not to be put off. "Let's go out on the street," he suggested, "and be really nice to a dog, and offer it biscuits, and—"

"Not my malted milks!" squealed Bryan.

"... offer it *other* biscuits," continued Icky, "and see if it will help us just for one night."

Bryan was not convinced. But as he was even more scared of ghosts than dogs, he had to go along with it. "Just leave the talking to me," he said.

The three mates set off down the road, looking nervously about. It wasn't long before they caught sight of a fox terrier, hanging about on the street corner chewing gum. It was unusual to see a dog on its own, so the three mates decided to seize their chance.

"Now listen and learn," said Bryan, "as I give a Masterclass in the Art of Talking to Dogs."

Bryan hailed the terrier with a friendly wave. "Hello, there!" he called.

The terrier focused its eyes on the approaching humans, but did not reply.

"Lovely day!" said Bryan, brightly.

The fox terrier stopped chewing. "Want to make something of it?" he snapped.

"I try to make something of every day," replied Bryan.

The fox terrier spat his gum on the ground. "Is that right?" he grunted.

"Indeed," said Bryan. "By the way, I hope you don't mind me offering you a little tip, but if you wrap your gum in a little piece of foil and put it in your pocket, you won't leave those unsightly blotches all over the pavement, which can also become stuck on the soles of one's shoes."

There was a long silence, while the terrier's ears slowly flattened and Stinky said a silent prayer.

"It is important to think of other people," added Bryan.

A little foam appeared at the corner of the terrier's mouth. "I'm a dog!" he barked. "I'm not a *people!*"

Bryan held up his hands like railway buffers. "Fair enough," he said. "Respect is due, pooch."

"What did you call me?" growled the terrier.

Bryan clammed up. The situation was looking quite unpromising, so Icky decided to put a quick end to it. "I think the word he used," said Icky, "was *mentalist.*"

The terrier's eyes came out like bloodshot gobstoppers.

"Run!" cried Icky.

The three mates hared back towards the house, the boiling mad terrier snapping at their heels. Luckily, the three mates were pretty good at running from dogs, because they'd had lots of practice. They fell into the House of Fun, slammed the door, then waited till the furious scratching died down.

"What did you say that for, Icky?" said Bryan. "I was just about to win him round."

"If you say so, Bryan," replied Icky.

"One thing's for sure," said Stinky. "Getting a

talking dog is Out of the Question."

They all sat down to ponder, except Icky didn't like pondering, so decided to get an idea straight away. "I know!" he said. "We get a dog from the Old Days, before they could talk."

"How are we going to do that?" said Bryan, but even as he said it, he realised.

"The Time Travel Garage!" they all cried.

Chapter Four

In the Time Travel Garage sat the Time Travel van, and it was not hard to decide who was going in it. Someone had to guard the malted milk biscuits.

"Are we nearly there yet?" asked Icky impatiently.

"We haven't got in the van yet, Icky," said Stinky.

"That's true," said Icky.

Icky and Stinky climbed into the Time Travel van, which was a fairly ordinary-looking van, resting on four fairly ordinary-looking piles of bricks. Then Icky twisted the ignition key, the dashboard turned itself inside out, metal shields came up over the windows, and suddenly everything was well sci-fi.

"Don't forget your seat-belt!" warned Stinky.

"No fear," said Icky. "I don't want to turn into a ninety-year-old man again."

Icky put on his seat-belt, which was a tight fit, as his pockets were full of chicken bits in case he got hungry.

"When shall we set the time-slider for?" asked Stinky.

"Before the Spoonheads came," replied Icky.

"What about 1487?" suggested Stinky.

"That'll do," said Icky.

Stinky set the time control, Icky pressed the big green button, and the two great mates hurtled backwards through time at three zillion orgs a gooby-second. Stinky offered Icky a peppermint and a join-the-dots fun-puzzle, mainly to stop him asking "Are we nearly there?" ten times a minute. But the van was working well for once, and the journey really didn't take that long. The whirrs and the rattles died down, the thousand little lights went out, and Icky eagerly threw open the door.

"Ooo," he said. "We're in a forest."

Icky and Stinky climbed out of the van. They were indeed in a forest, with various birds twittering, and, in the distance, a long lonely howl.

"Was that … a wolf?" asked Icky.

"Wolves died out years ago," replied Stinky.

"We're in years ago," Icky pointed out.

"Oh yes," replied Stinky.

Suddenly there was a rustling in the undergrowth, shouts, barks, and clopping hooves. A bunch of men appeared, dressed in rough old woollen garments. Two of them carried a long wooden box, a bit like a coffin. Another held two snarling hounds on a leash.

Icky was made up. The Time Travel Van had obviously landed right on the bull's-eye. "Hi!" he trilled. "We're from the future. Can we have one of your dogs?"

The men stood open-mouthed, and seemed unable to answer. But just then a further man rode his horse into view. This was a very different man, wearing a big red padded jacket, puffed-up breeches, and a baggy flat hat with a feather in it.

Icky and Stinky weren't sure who this man was, but he was obviously a major poser.

"Who are these boys?" he snapped.

"I dunno, sire," replied the dog-man. "Look like a pair of jesters."

The posey man rode his horse right up to Icky and Stinky. He actually smelled quite stinky himself, though with a hint of rosewater.

"Have you seen a wolf, jesters?" he asked.

"We did hear one," said Stinky.

"Not far off," added Icky.

"Aha," said the posey man. "Then we'll set the trap here."

The rough men with the wooden box laid it down on the turf.

"Get to it, men," said the posey man. "You know what to do."

The rough men began collecting branches and bracken, building it into a high circle about two metres across. Meanwhile the posey man inspected the Time Travel van with a curious eye.

"What is this infernal caravan?" he asked.

"It's not a caravan," replied Stinky, "it's a Time Travel machine."

"We've come from the future to get a dog," added Icky. "Do you know where we can get one?"

The posey man laughed gently. "You certainly are a fine pair of jesters!" he scoffed.

"No, really," insisted Icky. "We do want a dog."

"No one here will give you a dog, jester," replied the posey man. "Unless, that is, you want a wolf!"

The posey man laughed, and the rough men all laughed along with him.

"Are you going to trap a wolf?" asked Icky eagerly.

The posey man leaned closer. His breath was not pleasant. "They do say," he murmured, "'tis the last wolf in England."

"We'll have it," said Icky.

"Will we?" said Stinky.

"Why not?" said Icky. "A wolf's just like a dog."

"Is it?" said Stinky.

"I will make a deal with you," said the posey man.

"Fire away, boss," replied Icky.

The posey man frowned. "My name is Lord Blunderpant," he growled.

"Oh," said Stinky, disappointed. "I thought you might be king."

"That is treason talk!" cried the posey man. "Long live King Henry!"

"Long live King Henry!" cried the rough men.

"Wow," said Icky. "Is that Henry the Eighth?"

"Henry the Seventh, actually," replied Lord Blunderpant. "The one with the six wives comes next."

There was a short and slightly confused pause.

"So what is this deal, Lord Blunderpant?" asked Icky.

"Let me explain our little trap," replied Lord Blunderpant. He leapt down from his horse and began to prowl round the wall of branches in his great swollen breeches. "The wolf cannot enter this den," he said, "except by one route." Lord Blunderpant indicated the long wooden box. "However," he continued, "the moment he enters the trap, his weight will trigger a spring, and gates will snap shut at both ends. Ha!"

"Ha!" cried the rough men.

Icky didn't quite get it. "But why does the wolf want to get in to the den?" he asked.

"To get to the bait, of course," replied Lord Blunderpant.

"What bait?" asked Icky.

Lord Blunderpant laid a fancy gloved hand on Icky's shoulder. "You remember," he purred, "I offered you a deal?"

"Hmm?" said Icky.

"Can you guess what that deal might be?" asked Lord Blunderpant.

Icky pondered for a moment. "You wouldn't want *me* to be the bait, by any chance?" he asked.

"You're very sharp, for a jester," replied Lord Blunderpant.

"Hmm," said Icky, "and we get to keep the wolf, do we?"

"That is the deal," replied Lord Blunderpant.

"OK," said Icky. "I'll do it."

"Are you sure, Icky?" asked Stinky nervously.

"It'll be fun!" said Icky. "Besides, what can possibly go wrong?"

At this, there was a lot of coughing amongst the rough men.

"Did it work the last time?" asked Stinky.

"Last time?" repeated Lord Blunderpant. "What last time?"

Stinky's face fell, while Icky beamed more merrily than ever. "I'm a guinea-pig!" he trilled.

This puzzled the rough men, because this was 1487, and guinea-pigs hadn't been invented yet.

"The trap will work perfectly," declared Lord Blunderpant reassuringly. "And even if the wolf does get through, which of course he won't, I'm sure he won't bother with this little runt! He's nothing but a bag of bones!"

The men all laughed.

"Am not!" said Icky, puffing out his chest.

The men laughed even more.

"Where do I sit?" barked Icky in his most manly voice.

Lord Blunderpant guided Icky to the centre of the wall of greenery, where he sat cross-legged with a big tough look on his face. The trap was pushed into the gap in the wall. Now there was no sign of Icky, just a shout of, "See you later, Stinks!" which brought a lump to Stinky's throat.

"Night approaches fast," said Lord Blunderpant. "Our friend will not be long in coming,"

The rough men sprinkled half a bucket of fresh hog's blood on to the ground, just to make sure wolfie would take interest. Then they retreated to a safe hidey-hole, well away from the scene, taking Stinky with them.

The sun began to set and Icky began to get restless. He nibbled away at the chicken bones he'd brought with him, but when the chicken had gone, there really was nothing interesting to do. For a while he tried playing I-Spy, but it's not easy to play I-Spy by yourself, so he started to study the wolf-trap. It looked sturdy enough, but did it really work?

For the first time Icky began to worry. It wasn't normally Icky's nature to worry, but then he was always up and doing, and never had time to dwell on things. Now, as the minutes turned to hours, he had *plenty* of time to dwell on things – things like getting eaten by a wolf.

"Maybe I could *test* the trap," he thought to himself.

Icky got down on his knees and pressed one hand gently on to the floor of the trap.

Nothing happened.

"Guess that's not enough weight," Icky muttered.

Icky pressed both hands into the trap.

Nothing happened.

"Still not enough weight, maybe," murmured Icky.

Icky began to crawl, slowly and cautiously, inside the trap. Something in the back of his mind told him this *might* not be a good idea, but something in the front of his mind said *Go, Icky!*, and that thing was a lot louder.

Icky edged his way, bit by bit, right into the centre of the trap.

And then ...
... CLA-A-A-NG!

"Frabjous!" said Icky. "It *does* work!"

Icky's joy did not last long. It suddenly dawned on him that possibly, just possibly, he might not be able to get out again.

Icky pushed hard against the door at the end of the trap. It didn't budge.

Icky gave the door a kick. It still didn't budge.

Icky hammered the door with both fists, repeatedly, for about five minutes. That didn't work either.

At this point Icky heard an excited cry: "We've got him!" Footsteps came thundering through the woods.

Icky was in big trouble.

Icky decided to stay very still and quiet.

Stinky, meanwhile, was struggling to keep up with the others as they raced back over the bracken. He arrived just as Lord Blunderpant was leaping from his horse, then up on to the trap, arms held high.

"Today," he cried, "is a day which will go down in history! The day we rid this land for ever of the wolf!"

The rough men cheered, though they didn't

seem *quite* as happy as Lord Blunderpant, and were probably just keeping in his good books.

"Excuse me," said Stinky, "but can we see if Icky is all right?"

"Icky?" repeated Lord Blunderpant. "Ah yes! The bait!"

Lord Blunderpant instructed the men to tear down the wall of branches. Stinky waited eagerly for his great mate to appear. Except, of course, Icky never did appear. All that appeared, there in the centre of the circle, was a small pile of bones.

"Icky!" gasped Stinky.

"Zounds!" said Lord Blunderpant. "How did that happen?"

Icky, of course, could have explained everything, and might have done so if he wasn't afraid of being boiled in oil or getting his head chopped off. Icky sat tight and waited as Lord Blunderpant paced about the trap, thinking hard.

"I think I have it," he said. "Being poorly fed, the wolf in question was unusually light in weight. So light, in fact, that he failed to set off the trap on the way in. Whereas, on the way out, he was considerably heavier, having had … how can I put it? … a good feed."

The rough men agreed that this was exactly what had happened, and one of them helpfully collected the bones into a small rag pouch and handed them to Stinky. "There you go, mucker," he said. "We said he was a bag of bones."

Their peal of laughter echoed round the wood. Stinky held the little bag between his fingers and felt the same terrible emptiness he'd felt when Icky was carried off by a flying dinosaur. Except that time Icky had escaped, whereas this time he was most certainly gone for ever.

Actually Icky really had gone by now, in a sense. Being tired, and actually quite warm and cosy, he'd dropped off to sleep. This was quite common for Icky. He was a bit like a firecracker. When he was alight he really was alight, and when he was out, he really was out. Nothing stirred him, not even the rough men picking up the trap and slamming it down in the back of the Time Travel Van, ready for Stinky's sad journey home.

Chapter Five

"Well?" said Bryan excitedly.

"Well what?" replied Stinky.

"Did you get the dog?"

Stinky slumped on to the kitchen stool. "Kind of," he mumbled.

"How can you kind of get a dog?" asked Bryan.

"It's more of a wolf," replied Stinky. "In fact, it is a wolf."

Bryan thought about this. "Does it bite?" he asked.

Stinky's head sank. "Yes," he said. "It bit Icky."

"Badly?" asked Bryan.

"Very badly," replied Stinky.

"How badly is very badly?" asked Bryan.

"This badly," replied Stinky. He shook the little

bag of bones out on to the kitchen table.

"W-what's that?" stammered Bryan.

"That's Icky," replied Stinky.

Bryan said nothing. He took a few deep breaths, walked calmly to the cupboard, and took out his packet of malted milks. Then he sat down opposite Stinky, nibbling damply on the edge of a biscuit and making a muffled num-num hummy-type sound.

"I'm upset," said Stinky.

"What about?" said Bryan. He finished the first biscuit and started on the second one.

The num-nummy sound was getting louder and quite disturbing. Soon it was too much for Stinky to bear.

"I think we should get the wolf out," he said.

Bryan looked alarmed.

"It's what Icky would have wanted," added Stinky.

Bryan looked no less alarmed. "What if it bites us?" he asked.

"Well, we *could* leave it in the box," suggested Stinky.

"What's the good of a wolf in a box?" asked Bryan. "It can't see ghosts if it's in a box."

"That's a point," said Stinky.

"On second thoughts," said Bryan. "Maybe it can. Maybe it can use its sixth sense."

"Maybe," said Stinky, who wasn't sure what the first five senses were, let alone the sixth one.

"We'll put the box in the kitchen," said Bryan. "Near the biscuits."

With a heavy heart, Stinky returned to the Time Travel Van, and with a heavy box, he and Bryan returned to the kitchen. The box was placed in the middle of the floor, just below the biscuit cupboard.

"Are you sure there's a wolf in there?" asked Bryan. "It's keeping very quiet."

"Well, *something*'s in there," said Stinky. "And it must be a wolf, unless …"

"Unless what?"

"Unless … something else ate Icky."

Bryan reached for the malted milks. The two housemates sat in a quiet depression for a few minutes, almost silent except for the nibbling and num-nummy noises.

"Let's go to bed," said Bryan, eventually. "If we hear it howl, we'll know it's a wolf, and if it starts making strange whiney noises, we'll know it's seen a ghost."

It was the middle of the night when Icky finally woke up. He immediately knew he was back in the House of Fun because, even in the box, he could sense the house's special atmosphere. Icky was very good on atmospheres, partly because he had no sense of smell.

Note from Blue Soup:
The Spoonheads had been amazed to discover that each house on Earth had its own smell. There was

76

only one house-smell on the Spoonheads' planet, mainly because there was only one house, which everybody lived in. All the house-smells on Earth seemed extremely strange to the Spoonheads, but then they also seemed extremely strange to all humans, except the ones who lived in each particular house.

The smell of the House of Fun was surprisingly pleasant. That was because I provided a kind of underfloor air conditioning which ran beneath the entire crust of the Earth and mingled with the buildings to create homely air-cocktails. In the case of the House of Fun this was like warm garlic bread mixed with fresh rainy pavements and parma violets, with just a hint of Stinky's pants. No air-conditioning was strong enough to cover that smell.

Icky rapped hard on the inside of the box. "Stinky!" he called.

There was no answer.

Icky rapped again. "Bryan!" he called.

Still no answer.

Icky gave a third, much harder, rap. "It's Icky!"

he cried. "Let me out of here!"

At this point, the kitchen door gave a creak.

"Stinky?" murmured Icky.

No footsteps came into the room. But something did. Something that made a strange swishing sound, like curtains being dragged over a marble floor.

Exactly the sound Dronezone had described.

"Who's that?" said Icky.

The noise stopped. For a moment there was silence. Then the swishing began again, except in the opposite direction, and slightly faster. Eventually it faded to nothing, at which point Icky began shouting at the top of his voice: "Stinky! Bryan! Get up quick!" But there was still no response from the housemates.

Not knowing what else to do, Icky tipped back his head and howled.

Upstairs, Bryan sat bolt upright in bed. His first thought was that the wolf had escaped, so he armed himself with an umbrella and went to fetch Stinky. Together they crept downstairs to the kitchen, where they were relieved to find the wolf-trap intact, and no sign of a slavering beast.

"I swear I heard a howl," said Bryan.

"That was me," said the wolf-trap.

Bryan leapt back, quivering like a leaf. "The b-box!" he stammered. "It s-spoke!"

"Let me out, will you?" said the wolf-trap.

"W-what are you?" stammered Bryan.

"I'm an Icky!" replied the wolf-trap.

"Icky?" cried Stinky. "But your ... your bones are on the kitchen table."

"What?" said Icky.

"You're ... you're dead," said Stinky.

"Only my right arm," said Icky, "and that's cos I've been sleeping on it."

"I don't understand," said Stinky.

"What?" said Icky.

"Anything," said Stinky.

"As usual," said Icky. "Now can you let me out?"

Stinky moved towards the box, but Bryan held him back. "How do we know it's not a wolf pretending to be Icky?" he asked.

"Wolves couldn't talk in 1066," said Stinky, "or whenever it was."

"But now it's in Modern Times," said Bryan. "Maybe it can talk, now it's in Modern Times."

"That's a thought," said Stinky, who was always impressed by Thoughts.

"Let's ask it a question," said Bryan. "A question only Icky could answer, like 'What is your mother's maiden name?'"

"OK," said Stinky. "Can you think of a question like that?"

"What about 'What is your mother's maiden name?'" suggested Bryan, with a tired sigh.

"That's a good one," said Stinky.

"Thing in the box," pronounced Bryan. "What is your mother's maiden name?"

"Attabangawallabooga," replied Icky.

There was a short silence.

"What *is* Icky's mother's maiden name?" asked Bryan.

"Search me," replied Stinky.

"OK," said Bryan. "Now let's ask it a question which only Icky could answer, to which we *also* know the answer."

"That's an even better idea," said Stinky.

Bryan began to um and ah, but unfortunately, he knew lots about history, maths and geography, but next to nothing about his housemates. Bryan just couldn't think of a question to ask Icky.

"You think of a question, Stinky!" he snapped. "I don't see why I should do all the thinking all of the time!"

Stinky was daunted by the sudden responsibility, but after a few minutes, came up with an idea. "I'll ask him what is the funniest book he's ever read," he said.

"Ha!" scoffed Bryan. "Icky doesn't read books!"

"Thing in the box!" pronounced Stinky. "What is the funniest book you've ever read?"

"Bryan's diary," came the reply.

"Eh?" said Bryan.

"That's Icky!" cried Stinky. He busily pushed and pulled at the door on the end of the trap, till Icky came flying out like a jack-in-the-box, then went bouncing round the room in a jig of celebration. Stinky gave him his biggest hug and Bryan gave him his biggest scowl.

"I thought the wolf had eaten you!" cried Stinky.

"Nah!" said Icky. "I ate the wolf!"

Bryan was still scowling. "I don't have a diary," he growled. "It must be a fake."

"Never mind that!" trilled Icky. "I heard the ghost! It was in this room!"

"Are you sure, Icky?" asked Stinky.

"Positive!" said Icky. "The door creaked, then there was a swishy noise, just like Dronezone said!"

"Hmm," said Bryan, unimpressed. "If it was a

ghost, why did it need to open the door?"

"Maybe it just wanted to," replied Icky.

"Ghosts don't open doors," said Bryan.

Suddenly Icky pointed to the floor. "Look!" he cried. "A trail!"

Stinky and Bryan looked down. Sure enough, there was a damp line on the kitchen floor, like a wet cat had been dragged along it. The line went all the way to Bryan's biscuit tin.

"No-o-o-o!" cried Bryan. He seized the tin, ripped it open, and counted furiously. "Two more gone!" he howled.

"I know!" said Icky. "Let's follow the trail back where it came from!"

"Good thinking, Icky," said Stinky.

The three housemates began to follow the damp line out of the kitchen and back along the hall. Bryan was still suspicious. "If either of you did this," he said, "you'd better clear it up before Tarquin comes round."

Icky and Stinky stopped dead. "Tarquin?" they both asked. "Who's Tarquin?"

"My new friend," replied Bryan smugly.

"You've got a friend?" said Stinky, amazed.

"Well, not exactly a friend," replied Bryan. "More of a fan."

Icky and Stinky were all ears, which was exactly what Bryan wanted. He made the most of a long dramatic pause before explaining further. "It was while you were time-travelling," he announced. "I went out for a walk and heard my name being called. A very intelligent young man ran up to me and asked if I was Bryan Brain from Superchild Head Challenge on Channel P, which, of course, I was. We had a pleasant and interesting conversation, after which I invited him round for tea and biscuits."

Bryan finished his explanation, folded his arms, and waited for further questions.

"Right," said Icky. "Back to the trail."

Icky and Stinky set off up the stairs, then down the first floor landing, till they came to the door at the far end.

"The trail stops here," said Icky.

"What door is this?" asked Stinky.

"The Undersea World of Uncle Nero Bathroom," replied Icky.

"You mean you've *never* used the bathroom?" gasped Bryan, who'd just caught up.

Stinky thought for a moment. "I think I went to the toilet here once," he said.

"But there isn't a toilet in this room," said Bryan.

"In that case," said Stinky, "it was definitely here."

Bryan was horror-struck. Icky was more interested in the door. "It's locked!" he cried.

"It can't be!" said Bryan. But it was.

"That's it then," said Icky. "The ghost's in there."

"We'll have to smash it down," said Stinky.

"We're not smashing down any doors!" replied Bryan. "What will Tarquin think, coming to a house with smashed-down doors?"

"Blow Tarquin," said Icky, except he didn't really say "blow".

"Why don't we just use the Atomic Transmuter?" suggested Bryan.

"The Atomic Transmuter?" asked Icky. "What's an Atomic Transmuter?"

Bryan cleared his throat. "The Atomic Transmuter," he began, "sometimes known as the Nuclear Metashifter, was invented in the year—"

"Ah yes," said Icky quickly. "I remember now. Let's get it."

Bryan led the way to the Living Living Room, avoiding the clutches of a particularly aggressive

armchair. There in the corner was a tall oblong object about the size of a phone kiosk, except this kiosk had curvy shapely edges, a bit like it was melting.

Stinky had never noticed the object before, and Icky had always thought it was a phone kiosk.

"What does it do?" asked Stinky.

"According to the instructions," replied Bryan, "it transmits one through Space, rather as the Time Travel Van transmits one through Time. It does this by transforming one's Molecules into pure Energy, then re-forming them into Mass in the Place of One's Desire. But it can only do this over distances of half a metre or less. We will therefore have to place the Transmuter next to the bathroom door."

The three housemates duly carried the kiosk up the stairs and into position.

"So," said Stinky. "Who's going in?"

"Whose idea was it?" asked Icky.

"Are you joking?" said Bryan. "I'm not going in that!"

"Suit yourself," said Icky. "We'll just have to tell *Tarquin* what a scaredycat you are."

Bryan was flummoxed. "It always ends up as me!"

he snorted. Sulkily, he climbed inside the kiosk and began searching it with extreme care.

"What are you doing that for, Bryan?" asked Stinky.

"Nothing else must be in the Transmuter once it goes into operation," replied Bryan. "If, for example, there were a small spider in there, its atoms would become mingled with my own, and I would therefore become part human, part spider."

"Frabjous!" said Icky. "Let's do it."

"It's not a laughing matter," replied Bryan. He completed his inspection and climbed into the kiosk. "The next time you see me, I shall be inside the bathroom. Except, of course, you won't see me, until I open the door."

With that, Bryan locked himself into the kiosk, and the dangerous operation began.

Chapter Six

Note from Blue Soup:
This is another one of those chapters which simply carry on from where we left off. The last one was just getting too long.

There was a yell of triumph from behind the bathroom door: "It worked!" But Bryan's joy did not last long. The yell of triumph was followed by a spine-chilling cry of horror.

"The ghost's got Bryan!" yelled Icky. He hammered frantically on the door, which, to his surprise, came open.

Now it was Icky's turn to be horrified.

Something very dramatic had happened to Bryan, or more exactly, his head. Bryan's head had always been quite big, but now it was stretched out into a huge flat rectangle, a bit like a plasma screen in the Days of Olde. Pinholes were evenly spaced all over it, and a bobbly pattern ran round the edge. The texture of his skin had changed as well. Before, it was quite taut and shiny. Now it was kind of ... crumbly.

"W-what happened?" stammered Icky.

"The biscuit ..." panted Bryan. "... I forgot the biscuit in my pocket ..."

"Y-you mean ..." began Icky.

"Yes!" cried Bryan. "I am ... half human, half biscuit!"

It was almost too awful to take in.

"Would you like a cup of tea?" suggested Stinky.

"No I would not!" cried Bryan. "Have you

seen what cups of tea *do* to biscuits?"

"Fair point," said Stinky.

Icky's eyes were fixed on the bobbly bits round the outside of Bryan's head. He was still horrified, but at the same time, a bit fascinated. "Can I try a bit?" he asked.

"No, you cannot try a bit!" snapped Bryan.

A gust of wind blew from somewhere, and a small shower of crumbs blew away from Bryan's head. "I'm crumbling away!" he cried. "Do something!"

"We could pour glue over your head," suggested Icky.

"Then I wouldn't be able to breathe!" said Bryan.

Icky vaguely remembered a lesson about plaster masks, back in the days when young people went to school. "Put straws in your nostrils," he suggested.

Another wind blew. A few more crumbs showered down. "Do it then!" squealed Bryan.

The housemates went to work. Icky hurried downstairs to find some glue, while Stinky found two straws for Bryan's nostrils, and an empty bog roll for his mouth, just to make doubly sure. But as they waited for Icky to return, Bryan began to feel an odd tingly sensation, and could sense his ears coming closer together.

"It's wearing off!" he cried.

Sure enough, Bryan's head was slowly returning to its normal shape, while the biscuit was re-forming in his pocket.

"Thank heaven for that," said Bryan. "It was only temporary."

At this point Icky's footsteps came clattering up the stairs.

"It's OK, Icky!" shouted Stinky. "Bryan's coming back to—"

Stinky never got to finish his sentence. Icky had crashed into the room like a charging rhino and emptied an entire bucket of glue over Bryan's head.

Bryan's arms windmilled wildly. He was building up for one of his foulest oaths. "You ... you ... perfect oaf!" he cried, except it got muffled by the toilet roll tube and sounded like a train announcement.

"I'll get it off, Bryan," said Stinky.

"No! Stay away!" cried Bryan, but it was too late. All the maggots, flies and other debris from Stinky's hair got stuck fast in the glue. In a panic, Stinky seized a bog-brush and made to sweep it all away, except the bog-brush also get stuck fast and dangled from Bryan's head like a novelty earring.

"Asses!" cried Bryan. "Nincompoops!" He managed to gouge away enough glue to reveal one staring eye, which settled on the nearby door. In sheer frustration, he brought back his head and nutted it full force. This, of course, was a big mistake. Icky had used the best contact adhesive, perfect for fixing metal to glass, plastic to pottery, and heads to doors.

"Help!" cried Bryan. "Get me off this door!"

This was not an easy operation. Icky fetched the house toolbox, took out a saw, then climbed on a chair behind Bryan and sawed a neat circle in the wood, which remained firmly stuck to Bryan's forehead.

"Just think," said Icky. "If we'd done that in the first place, we wouldn't have needed the Transmuter, and none of this would have happened."

Bryan gave a low growl, then stamped out of the room and down the stairs.

"Bryan!" cried Stinky. "Where are you going?"

"To get a blimming biscuit!" yelled Bryan, except he didn't really say 'blimming'.

Just then there was a knock at the front door.

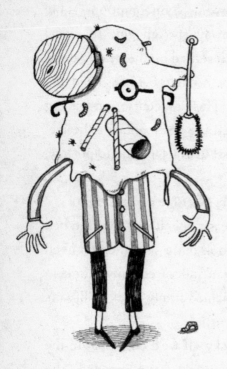

"*Yes?*" snapped Bryan, flinging it open.

A neatly dressed young man backed away in horror.

"Tarquin!" cried Bryan. "Tarquin, it's me, Bryan!"

Tarquin turned on his heels and fled down the steps.

"Wait, Tarquin!" yelled Bryan, giving chase.

Tarquin did not look much of a sprinter, but the sight of Bryan obviously inspired him. He was down the road before you could say Superchild Head Challenge.

"Tarquin!" called Bryan. "Don't you want the tea and biscuits?" There was no one to hear him.

"Never mind, Bryan," said Stinky, and Bryan trudged back into the house. "We're still your friends."

"Tarquin was more than a friend," moaned Bryan. "He was a fan."

Bryan slumped down on to the hall table. He looked impossibly sad, or as sad as is possible when maggots, flies, a bogbrush and a piece of door are stuck to your face.

"Tell you what, Bry," said Icky. "Now the glue's set, I reckon we could peel it off."

"Peel it off?" moaned Bryan. "How?"

"I reckon," said Icky, "if we get hold of it from the bottom, we could pull it off like a pullover."

There was a brief sigh from Stinky, as he remembered the time he'd pulled off Old Smelly. What a mistake that had been.

"Be *very* careful then," warned Bryan.

"Come on, Stinky," said Icky. They took hold of the bottom end of the glue, which was quite rubbery and more like a wetsuit than a pullover.

But sure enough, as they pulled upwards, it did begin to lift off in an inside-out manner.

"Careful!" warned Bryan, but his words were muffled, because the rubber jumper was just passing his mouth, dragging the bogroll tube with it. Another pull, and Bryan's nose appeared. Then things got a bit more difficult. The rubber jumper was jammed.

"One big yank," said Icky, "and it'll come clean off."

Icky braced his leg against one side of the door frame. Stinky braced his leg against the other.

"Are you sure this is a good idea, Icky?" asked Stinky.

"Sure I am!" said Icky.

"What's going on?" quivered Bryan.

"Ready, Stinky?" said Icky. "One …"

"Two …"

"THREE!"

"**AIEEEEEEEEEEEEEEEEEEE!**" said Bryan.

"Oh dear," said Stinky.

"Hmm," said Icky, scratching his head. "Didn't Bryan used to have hair?"

"And eyebrows," said Stinky.

"W-what have you done?" bleated Bryan. Fearfully, he brought his hand up to the top of his head, which, as you may have gathered, was bald as a pool ball. "My lovely hair!" he cried.

"And your eyebrows," added Stinky.

"Never mind, Bryan," said Icky. "At least you've still got your eyelashes." He peered more closely. "Oh no. They've gone as well."

With his favourite school cap back on his head, Bryan didn't look too bad. It was time to be a brave soldier and get back on the trail of the biscuit thief. The three great mates made their way back to the Undersea World of Uncle Nero Bathroom to examine the evidence.

The Undersea World of Uncle Nero Bathroom was not much like any other bathroom. For a start, there wasn't a bath in it. The centre of the room was occupied by a crater about two metres wide, in which a pool of warm sapphire water slowly rose and fell, occasionally gushing a few metres into the air like a geyser. There was a channel running into the crater from the shower, which was more like a waterfall, cascading down along the full length of the far wall. The walls and the floor were made out of a sparkly marbly rock, and nothing was flat and straight, but curvy and wavy, as if it had been shaped by the sea. It was Icky's favourite room, especially at night, when all the laser lights came on and wondrous dusk-plants grew out of the walls.

There was, however, nowhere to hide.

"The ghost must have gone in the pool," said Icky.

The three mates studied the floor closely. The trail of water was getting faint now, but sure enough, it led to the edge of the crater.

"Hmm," said Stinky. "How deep is it?"

"Search me," said Bryan.

"Oh," said Stinky cheerily. "You don't bath either."

"I shower," snapped Bryan.

"I've been in it," said Icky. "I was playing tig with Orfor and fell in."

Note from Blue Soup:

You will find Orfor the eagle in Crazy Party at the House

98

of Fun, but unfortunately no record of the games he played with Icky.

"Did you find out how deep it was?" asked Stinky.

"I never reached the bottom," replied Icky.

"Wow," said Stinky. "That's deep."

"We need a submarine," said Bryan.

Icky and Bryan thought about submarines a while, and Stinky thought about thinking.

"Wetsuits!" said Icky suddenly.

"What wetsuits?" said Bryan.

"I've seen them in the Dressing-up Room!" said Icky. "And flippers! And oxygen!"

"This is starting to sound like fun," said Stinky.

"It's not fun," said Bryan. "It's a Serious Investigation."

The three mates made their way to the Dressing-up Room, which, as we know, was full of all the costumes under the sun, and at least three costumes under the sea. Just as Icky had remembered, there were a whole row of wetsuits, with facemasks and flippers and even underwater radio mikes. Icky helped Stinky into his suit first, then strapped the oxygen tanks to his back.

Bryan and Icky then put their suits on, but at this point realised there was a problem.

"Where's the other oxygen tanks?" asked Bryan.

There were no other oxygen tanks. But Icky was not deterred. He had noticed a fire hose on the wall, and had had an idea.

"Hold tight," he said. "I'm going to make some slight alterations."

Icky went to work. As always, Icky worked at a hundred miles an hour, cutting and sticking and feeding bits of hosepipe all over the place. It wasn't long before he was done.

"There," he said. "Now we've all got oxygen."

"How does it work, Icky?" asked Stinky.

"Simple," said Icky. "You carry the tanks. The hosepipe comes out of the rear end of your suit, and into Bryan's facemask."

"Hold it right there," said Bryan.

"What's the problem?" said Icky.

"Have you forgotten," said Bryan, "the Pantomime Horse Incident?"

Bryan reminded Icky of the time Stinky was the front end of a panto horse, and made a solemn promise not to release personal gases while Bryan was in the back. It was a promise he had broken in no uncertain terms.

"The panto horse was a long time ago," said Icky. "This is a fresh start."

"It won't stay fresh for long," said Bryan.

"I swear I'll keep it in this time," said Stinky.

"You swore you'd keep it in last time," replied Bryan.

The three mates were at stalemate.

"Listen, Bryan," said Icky. "You've just got to trust Stinky this time. Otherwise we'll never catch the biscuit thief."

Bryan frowned.

"You do want to catch the biscuit thief, don't you?" said Icky.

Bryan had no choice. "All right," he said. "But if Stinky breaks his word this time, I will never ever trust either of you again!"

Chapter Seven

The three mates gazed into the depths of the house bath.

"We could get lost in there," said Stinky.

"Not if we hang on to the chain," replied Bryan. He pointed out the chrome chain which hung down into the water. At the end of that, no doubt, was the bath plug, and when they reached that, they were sure to be on the bottom.

"OK, everybody," said Icky. "Facemasks on."

Bryan paused. "You do remember your solemn oath, don't you, Stinky?" he asked.

"I do," replied Stinky.

"Let's go," said Icky.

Stinky led the way into the bath, followed by Bryan, followed by Icky. They sank slowly into the depths, going hand-over-hand down the bath-chain. The air supply worked perfectly, ensuring an excellent supply of fresh oxygen.

Down they went, and down, and down. A few fish began to appear – bright tropical ones, because after all, the bath water was quite warm.

"Bryan." It was Stinky's voice over the radio-mike.

"Yes?" snapped Bryan.

"I've got to warn you about something," said Stinky.

"W-what?" stammered Bryan.

"The chain gets a bit slippy down here," said Stinky.

"Oh," replied Bryan. "Right. Thank you."

Down they went, and down, and down. A whole seascape was opening out around them, full of coral, and anemones, and scooting schools of fish.

"Bryan." It was Stinky again.

"What now?" snapped Bryan.

"Something's coming out," said Stinky.

"W-what do you mean?" stuttered Bryan.

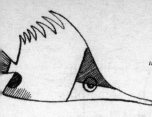

"From that rock down there," said Stinky. "I think it's an eel."

"Oh," said Bryan. "OK. I'll watch out for that."

At last the bottom of the bath came into sight, and the three mates came to a soft landing on a bed of pure white sand. They had arrived in an underwater paradise. Beside them was an arch of rock, and through that the white sand made a winding path through a grotto of coral dotted with sea-plants of every colour. Ornate and tiny fish flickered this way and that, like the finishing touches to a picture of perfect peace.

"Nature's great," mused Stinky.

"Nature's definitely one of the best things around," agreed Icky.

"Do you know," said Stinky, "I feel so relaxed, I could ..."

"What?" snapped Bryan.

"... sing," said Stinky. And indeed, he did hum a merry tune, as they set off down the winding path towards the vista of fantastic promise that lay at the end of it. There was a feeling that something great was about to happen – something monstrously powerful and unforgettable that none of them would ever forget.

And then … it happened.

The promise became a reality.

There before them stood the most majestic building they had ever seen – a towering underwater cathedral of a thousand colours. Whether it was natural or deliberate it was hard to say – it could have been a mixture of both, half-grown and half-built. The cathedral looked fantastically strong and yet impossibly delicate, with fishes flitting in and out of details as fine as lace.

"What is this thing?" asked Stinky, awe-struck.

"Let's go in and find out!" said Icky.

The three mates entered through an arch in the centre of the cathedral, only to find they were in a small chamber with barely room to move. As soon as they were all crammed tight in there, a gate came down across the arch. They were trapped.

Suddenly the water level began to fall.

"It's an air-lock!" cried Icky.

Bryan waited with bated breath as the water level reached the top of his head, then sank to the level of his nose. Any second now, and he would be able to remove the face-mask. Three centimetres ... two ...

... one ...

... zero.

Bryan removed his face-mask with a sigh of relief.

Note from Blue Soup:

I hope no one seriously thought Stinky was going to break his promise. If you are one of those sad people who enjoy cheap laughs about digestive gases, I strongly advise you to look elsewhere – for example, the other books about Stinky.

The last of the water drained out of the air-lock. Behind, a door creaked open. The three mates turned and entered a magnificent space, full of coral columns stretching ever upwards and walls of soft wavy marble, broken by epic windows which looked out on a magic aquarium of sea life.

Icky, Stinky and Bryan were stunned to silence. They paced with solemn slowness through the palace of light and life, wondering what frabjous underwater god could have inspired it.

The great cathedral was circular, and in the middle of that circle was a fantastic arrangement which looked like the luminous skeleton of a whale. When the three mates reached this, they saw within it three great chairs, the centre one larger than the others. The borders of the chairs were studded with silver stars, and in front of each was a bowl of tortoiseshell on a table of sea-worn timber.

In each bowl were a handful of malted milk biscuits.

"My biscuits!" cried Bryan, and his words boomed round the cathedral like a voice from the heavens. He rushed towards the nearest table, but Stinky grabbed his arm.

"Careful, Bryan," he warned. "We don't know what's going on here."

"But I need them!" cried Bryan.

"Maybe they know that," said Stinky.

"Stinky!" said Icky. "Look at the letters on the chairs!"

Stinky viewed the chairs more closely. Sure enough, each had a gold letter in the centre of the backrest. The one on the left said I, the one on the right said B, and the one in the centre said S.

"What do you think those letters mean?" asked Stinky.

"I'm Icky," said Icky. "He's Bryan, and you're Stinky."

Stinky nodded thoughtfully. "And?" he said.

"It's our initials, Stinky!" cried Icky. "The chairs must be for us!"

"Wow," said Stinky.

"Why haven't I got the big chair?" muttered Bryan.

"Let's sit on them!" said Icky.

Stinky approached the centre chair, then hesitated. "It looks too good to sit on," he said.

"Stinky," replied Icky. "It's meant for you. Sit on it."

Bryan decided to set an example by sitting on his own chair and starting on the biscuits. Icky followed, lounging back over the arms of his chair and striking a well smug pose. Finally, Stinky plucked up the courage to take his own seat.

At this very moment, or so it seemed, a brilliant light shone through the giant window high above the entrance to the cathedral. Whether it was the sun, or the brilliance of a thousand luminous fish, it was hard to say. But the three housemates found themselves shielding their eyes from the glare, almost blinded by it.

At this point there arose a sinister sound, echoing round the walls like organ music. It was a swishing sound, like curtains being dragged across a marble floor.

Icky sat up straight in his chair.

Bryan's teeth froze on his biscuit.

"W-who's that?" called Stinky.

The swishing was growing closer, moving up the aisle directly towards the three mates.

"I can't see!" hissed Stinky.

"Nor can I!" said Icky.

The swishing grew closer and closer, till it seemed it was almost upon them. Then, quite suddenly, there came a voice – a strange, flat, robot voice: **I have been expecting you.**

Icky, Stinky and Bryan sat as rigid as statues, too scared to move or speak.

111

Fear not, said the voice. **I am your friend.**

The three mates were not convinced. Then, however, the brilliant light began to dim a little, their eyes adjusted, and slowly they began to make out the form before them. At first it looked like some kind of dark, shaggy animal. But there was no head on this animal, or tail, or back legs even. Where its front paws should have been, there were just ragged, trailing ends. One of these ends seemed to be holding something – something like a computer keyboard.

Suddenly, another light dawned on Stinky.

"Old Faithful!" he cried. "Is it you?"

The ragged creature tapped away on the keyboard. **I have missed you, Stinky,** it said.

"I've missed you, Old Faithful!" cried Stinky.

"Is that my Burpitron text-to-voice vocal synth module?" said Bryan.

All possessions will be returned, replied the mangy jumper, **now my work is complete.**

"I don't understand," said Stinky.

I wanted to thank you, replied Old Faithful, **for giving me the Gift of Life.**

"The gift of life?" said Stinky. "How did I do that?"

Do you not remember, replied Old Faithful, **all those years ago, when your mother said to you, "If you do not wash that jumper, it will get up and walk?"**

"Oh yes," said Stinky. "I remember that now."

Your mother was right, replied Old Faithful.

"Wow," said Stinky.

"You're not really walking," said Icky. "You're crawling."

Indeed, replied Old Faithful. **I do not move**

well on land. But, quite by chance, I have discovered my true element. In the water I can move as smoothly and gracefully as the shark, the seal and the penguin.

"Did you build all this?" asked Bryan.

There was a robotic laugh. **This was all here before me,** replied Old Faithful. **I merely gave it a makeover.**

"How did you know we'd find it?" asked Icky.

Aha, replied Old Faithful.

Silence descended. There were so many questions to ask of Old Faithful, but only one that really mattered to Stinky. "Are you coming home?" he asked.

There was a long pause. **I'm sorry,** replied Old Faithful, **but I have my own life to lead now.**

Icky laid a hand on Stinky's shoulder. "Never mind, Stinky," he said. "There's plenty more fish in the sea."

"There's only one jumper," replied Stinky.

Maybe we could have a private moment, suggested Old Faithful.

It only took five or six minutes for Bryan and Icky to get the message. They retreated to a respectful distance while Old Faithful and Stinky sat on a driftwood table together. They talked for a long time, Stinky gently holding the frayed end of Old Faithful's arm. Stinky seemed to go through the whole range of emotions, but at the end they put their arms round each other, then Old Faithful made his way back down the aisle, becoming smaller and smaller till finally he vanished through the cathedral door. With a brave face, Stinky made his way over to his two great mates.

"He who binds to himself a Joy," he began, "Does the winged Life destroy. But he who kisses the Joy as it flies, lives in Eternity's Sunrise."

"Eh?" said Icky.

"Just something I learned from Old Faithful," said Stinky.

"Where's he gone?" asked Bryan.

"Look!" said Stinky. And at that moment, Old Faithful appeared outside the window,

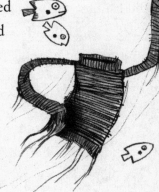

115

gliding through the water, twisting and turning effortlessly amongst the angel fish. He gave one last wave of his ragged arm, and was gone.

Chapter Eight

Icky and Stinky sat on their favourite tree-stumps, at the edge of the silver forest, looking down at the misty city below. It was autumn, their favourite season, and their feet were buried in leaves of copper and gold.

"I think this has been our best adventure so far," said Icky.

"The ending was a bit sad," said Stinky.

"But kind of happy too," said Icky.

"That's it," said Stinky. "Sad and happy."

He smiled weakly.

"Bryan had a bit of a rough time in this adventure," said Icky.

"Yes," agreed Stinky. "I was thinking we should get him something, like a new hat."

"That reminds me," said Icky.

Icky took the rucksack off his back, delved into it, and brought out a knotted grey jumper with a picture of a red panda on the back. "I found this in the Dressing-up Room," he said. "I thought you'd like it."

"Oh, cheers, Icky!" said Stinky. He took the jumper, but couldn't keep the sadness off his face. "It's not like Old Faithful," he said.

"No," said Icky. "It's New Faithful."

"That's it," said Stinky. "New Faithful."

"It'll become like Old Faithful in time," said Icky. "Once you've slept in it for a few years."

"I suppose I'll get used to it," said Stinky.

"It takes time," said Icky.

Stinky pulled New Faithful over his head. It smelled of clean wool and washing powder, but that didn't matter. It was warm and comforting, and it wasn't long before the first maggots had jumped off Stinky's hair and made themselves at home in it. Soon, like Icky, Stinky and Bryan, it would become part of *their* home, the always mysterious House of Fun.

Another title from Hodder Children's Books:

STINKY FINGER'S HOUSE OF FUN

Jon Blake

The Spoonheads have arrived in their space-hoovers and sucked up all the grown-ups! So Stinky and Icky will never have to change their underwear again.

In search of an Aim in Life, the two great mates head off to Uncle Nero's House of Fun. But soon they're being besieged by an army of pigs who want to make people pies!

They're going to need more than Icky's lucky feather and Stinky's smelly pants to save their crazy new home ...

Another title from Hodder Children's Books:

CRAZY PARTY AT THE HOUSE OF FUN

Jon Blake

The Spoonheads have sucked up all the grown-ups into their space zoo, so Stinky and Icky decide to invite all their friends to the greatest party ever.

But disaster strikes during a routine visit to the Brain Drain (to donate brains). Stinky and Icky lose a vital part of their memory! As party-time ticks ever closer, Stinky has to chase the Brain Drain van all the way to Planet Honk to get back their lost minds ...

Another title from Hodder Children's Books:

THE DEADLY SECRET OF DOROTHY W.

Jon Blake

When Jasmin wins a place at the Dorothy Wordsearch School for Gifted Young Writers, things look fishy. Who exactly is the mysterious Mr Collins?

How come Miss Birdshot, the wizened old housekeeper, is so incredibly strong?

And why do Jasmin's fellow pupils keep disappearing?

As Jasmin unravels Dorothy W.'s deadly secret, she finds herself literally writing for her life. Now, only the most brilliant story will help her survive!

'It's original and witty, full of amusing characterisation — a funny adventure story which credits its readers with intelligence.' Books for Keeps

Another title from Hodder Children's Books:

THE MAD MISSION OF JASMIN J.

Jon Blake

The last time Jasmin saw Dorothy Wordsearch, the awful author was being eaten by a monster.

So how come she's still writing stories?

It's time for Jasmin to investigate – helped, but mainly hindered, by her hyper sidekick Kevin Shilling.

And when Kevin is won over by a sinister new enemy, Jasmin will need all her wits to save him from a terrible fate …